Trash Heap
of Terror

ALSO BY JOE McGEE

NIGHT FRIGHTS
The Haunted Mustache
The Lurking Lima Bean
The Not-So-Itsy-Bitsy Spider

JUNIOR MONSTER SCOUTS
The Monster Squad
Crash! Bang! Boo!
It's Raining Bats and Frogs!
Monster of Disguise

JUNIOR MONSTER SCOUTS

#5 Trash Heap of Terror

By Joe McGee
Illustrated by Ethan Long

ALADDIN

NEW YORK   LONDON   TORONTO   SYDNEY   NEW DELHI

ALADDIN

An imprint of Simon & Schuster Children's Publishing Division
1230 Avenue of the Americas, New York, New York 10020
First Aladdin hardcover edition April 2022
Text copyright © 2022 by Joseph McGee
Illustrations copyright © 2022 by Ethan Long
Also available in an Aladdin paperback edition.
For information about special discounts for bulk purchases, please contact
Simon & Schuster Special Sales at 1-866-506-1949 or business@simonandschuster.com.
The Simon & Schuster Speakers Bureau can bring authors to your live event.
For more information or to book an event contact the Simon & Schuster Speakers Bureau
at 1-866-248-3049 or visit our website at www.simonspeakers.com.
Jacket designed by Karin Paprocki
Interior designed by Mike Rosamilia
The illustrations for this book were rendered digitally.
The text of this book was set in Centaur MT.
Manufactured in the United States of America 0322 FFG
2 4 6 8 10 9 7 5 3 1
Library of Congress Control Number 2021946864
ISBN 9781534487437 (hc)
ISBN 9781534487420 (pbk)
ISBN 9781534487444 (ebook)

FOR ANYONE WHO STOPS

to pick up litter when they see it—
thanks for taking a second to make
the world a cleaner, healthier space

· THE SCOUTS ·

VAMPYRA may be a vampire, but that doesn't mean she wants your blood. Gross! In fact, she doesn't even like ketchup! She loves gymnastics, especially cartwheels, and one of her favorite things is hanging upside down . . . even when she's *not* a bat. She loves garlic in her food and sleeps in past noon, preferring the nighttime over the day. She lives in Castle Dracula with her mom, dad (Dracula), and aunts, who are always after her to brush her fangs and clean her cape.

WOLFY and his family live high in the mountains above Castle Dracula, where they can get the best view of the moon. He likes to hike and play in the creek and gaze at the stars. He especially likes to fetch sticks with his dad, Wolf Man, and go on family pack runs, even if he has to put up with all of his little brothers and sisters. They're always howling when he tries to talk! Mom says he has his father's fur. Boy, is he proud of that!

 **FRANKY STEIN** has always been bigger than the other monsters. But it's not just his body that's big. It's his brain and his heart as well. He has plenty of hugs and smiles to go around. His dad, Frankenstein, is the scoutmaster, and one of Franky's favorite things is his well-worn Junior Monster Scout handbook. One day Franky is going to be a scoutmaster, like his dad. But for now . . . he wants a puppy. Dad says he'll make Franky one soon. Mom says Franky has to keep his workshop clean for a week first.

GLOOMY
WOODS

LAKE

VILLAGE

BARON VON
GRUMP'S HOUSE

Trash Heap
of Terror

CHAPTER
1

BARON VON GRUMP STARED AT THE LETTER in his hand.

"This can't be right," he said. "This can't be right at all."

"Caw?" asked Edgar, his pet crow.

"Yes, here!" said Baron Von Grump. "To this very place. To our windmill!"

"Caw?"

"When?" said Baron Von Grump. "Why, I haven't the slightest idea. She could show up at any moment. She could be almost here. She could be passing through the village at this very second!"

"Caw!" said Edgar. He flew to the windowsill and peered out over the village.

Baron Von Grump stared at the letter again.

"An extended stay," he moaned. "To visit the countryside."

He collapsed into his favorite chair and groaned.

"Caw?" asked Edgar.

"That's it!" said Baron Von Grump, jumping out of his seat. "That's exactly it, Edgar! We'll pack up and leave. We'll hang a sign on the door that says, 'Not home, gone away.' Why, she'll have no choice but to turn around and go right back to her noisy, busy, hustle-and-bustle city. Hurry, Edgar, we must be quick. There's no telling when she might—"

Three loud knocks at his front door interrupted him.

"Arrive," grumbled Baron Von Grump, falling back into his chair.

But wait, what about the Junior Monster Scouts? Where are they? Why are we reading about Baron Von Grump? This book series isn't called the Baron Von Grump series, is it? No, of course not! It's called the Junior Monster Scouts series, and that's who we really want to read about. What's that? You want to know who is knocking at Baron Von Grump's door? All in due time, but first let's see what our favorite Junior Monster Scouts are up to on this nice sunny day.

"Okay, Little Junior Monster Scouts," said Vampyra, "let's try the scout oath."

"Repeat after us," said Franky.

"After us," said Wolfy's little sister Fern and the rest of the cubs.

"No, repeat what we say," Wolfy said.

"What we say," said Fern and the cubs.

"No, repeat the oath," said Vampyra.

Fern scratched her head.

"But we don't know it," she said.

Wolfy rolled his eyes.

"That's what we're trying to teach you," he said.

"This is very confusing," said Fern.

As you can see, Vampyra, Franky, and Wolfy were trying very hard to teach the newly created *Little* Junior Monster Scouts the scout oath. Perhaps you and I could recite it together? After all, by reading these books, you are an honorary scout. Yes, of course you are! It doesn't matter if you don't have fur, or claws, or pointy teeth. What matters is that you are kind, and helpful, and follow all the other Scout Laws that are at the back of this book. But first, let's start with the oath. Ready? Okay, repeat after me:

I promise to be nice, not scary. To help, not harm. To always try to do my best. I am a monster, but I am not mean. I am a Junior Monster Scout!

2

BARON VON GRUMP DID NOT ANSWER his door right away. He hoped that if he ignored the knocking, whoever was at his door would go away.

Knock, knock, knock.

He knew exactly who was at his door.

KNOCK, KNOCK, KNOCK.

And he knew that she would *not* go away, no matter how much he hoped she would.

KNOCK, KNOCK, KNOCK.

But he tried anyway. It didn't work.

"Oh, cousin," called a voice from below Baron Von Grump's window. "I know you're in there! I've come such a long way to see you, and it would be very nice if you would OPEN THIS DOOR RIGHT NOW!"

Baron Von Grump jumped out of his seat. Edgar flew straight up into the rafters and bumped his head. Baron Von Grump rushed down the stairs and threw the door open. There, standing on his NOT WELCOME mat was none other than his cousin, the very frightening, always scowling, super-stern—

"Baroness Von Grumpier," said the baron, "how . . . nice . . . to see you."

Baron Von Grump smiled at her as best he could. It was really the tiniest of smiles.

No more than one twitch of one side of his lips. It was really the best he could do.

Baroness Von Grumpier did not smile back.

That's rather rude, don't you think? Most people at least smile back when you smile, even if it's a little smile. Let's try it. Is there anyone around you now? Try smiling at them. Tell them it's nice to see them. Did they smile back? They probably did. It's a *nice* thing to do. If they didn't, well . . . I'd keep your eye on them if I were you.

"Take this suitcase," said Baroness Von Grumpier. She thrust a large piece of luggage into Baron Von Grump's hands. "And this one. And this satchel. This trunk. These bags. And this box."

Baron Von Grump could not even see over the pile of bags and boxes and satchels and suitcases. Why, it was a wonder he could even fit through the door. But fit through the door he did, and Baroness Von Grumpier followed with empty hands. Almost empty. She held a large, warty, frowning toad in one hand.

"Croak," said the toad.

"I quite agree, Wilma," said Baroness Von Grumpier. "This place is even worse than it appears from the outside. You live in quite the dump, cousin."

Baron Von Grump gritted his teeth. He flared his nostrils. He tugged at his ears and pulled on his beard, but he did not say anything back. At least not anything that might make his cousin even crankier than she already was. He dared not do that.

Baron Von Grump knew better. Baroness Von Grumpier was known among all the Von Grumps as being the crankiest Von Grump there was.

Instead, he forced another smile, this one with a twitch of *both* corners of his lips.

"Care for some tea?" he said.

Baroness Von Grumpier's eyes narrowed, and her lip curled.

"I hate tea," she said.

"Milk?"

"I'd rather drink pond water," she sneered.

Baron Von Grump twisted the ends of his mustache. He was not feeling well at all.

CHAPTER 3

"SO WHAT ELSE ARE WE GOING TO do today?" asked Fern. Fern was Wolfy's little sister. She and the rest of the wolf cubs had just recently become *Little* Junior Monster Scouts. Little Junior Monster Scouts were Junior Monster Scouts in training. When they got bigger, they could be full scouts, just like Wolfy, Franky, and Vampyra! They had recently learned the scout oath. It had taken them several tries, but hey—practice makes perfect, right?

"Today," said Vampyra, "we are going to clean up the Crooked Trail."

"Someone has been littering," said Franky. He picked up a cheese wrapper and a tin can and dropped them into the trash bag he was carrying.

"Look at all this garbage!" said Wolfy. "Who would do this?"

"A monster!" said Fern. All the other cubs nodded and howled in agreement.

"You know *we* are monsters, right?" Wolfy asked.

"Oh yeah," said Fern.

"Maybe if we follow the trail of trash, we'll find out who's been littering," said Vampyra.

"Great idea!" said Franky.

Vampyra, Franky, and Wolfy led the way. Fern and the rest of the cubs followed. Every time they came to an old stinky sock, or a brown banana peel, or a wadded-up napkin, they stopped and picked it up. Fortunately for them, Franky's uncle, Igor Senior, and Franky's grandfather, Doctor Frankenstein, had made them windup garbage scoopers. All they had to do was turn the crank and scoop, scoop, scoop! The metal jaws swallowed up the trash and dropped it into their bags. No monster wanted to soil their paws on a slimy banana peel or stinky sock. Gross!

They did this all the way down the Crooked Trail, Junior Monster Scouts on

one side of the trail and Little Junior Monster Scouts on the other side. They found all kinds of junk that needed to be collected. Springs, old cans, apple cores, and broken shoelaces. But when they reached the beginning of the Gloomy Woods, the trash trail stopped.

"That's weird," said Wolfy.

"Guys, look," said Franky. He pointed to a pile of cheese crumbs on the side of the road.

"Who do we know who loves cheese more than anything?" Vampyra asked.

Do *you* know who loves cheese more than anything? Can you remember who is always chomping on cheese? I'll give you a hint. They have long whiskers and longer tails, and the answer rhymes with "bats."

You guessed it—rats!

"Something tells me that Boris and the rest of his crew are behind this," said Franky.

Boris was the lead rat. He and the other rats lived in the basement of Castle

Dracula, ever since the Junior Monster Scouts' first adventure and run-in with Baron Von Grump.

"Let's go find out," said Wolfy. "Follow me. I can sniff out their cheese tracks."

The cheese crumbs led Wolfy and the scouts away from the Crooked Trail, away from the Gloomy Woods, and out toward the edge of the cliffs.

Meanwhile . . . back in Baron Von Grump's windmill, the baron was having a very hard time. First he had put all of Baroness Von Grumpier's things upstairs. Her luggage and satchel and trunk and bags and box. Then Baroness Von Grumpier wanted them downstairs. Baron Von Grump moved her luggage and satchel and trunk and bags and box all back downstairs. Then back upstairs. Then back downstairs.

"I simply cannot make up my mind," said Baroness Von Grumpier.

"I noticed," said Baron Von Grump. He wiped several beads of sweat from his forehead.

"Croak," said Wilma.

"Yes, of course," said Baroness Von Grumpier. "All this moving and unpacking has made me awfully hungry. I wonder, cousin, do you have any cheese to snack on? That is what these villagers are known for, isn't it?"

Baron Von Grump was about to answer when Edgar settled on his shoulder.

"Caw, caw," said Edgar into Baron Von Grump's ear.

"Oh, you've outdone yourself, my feathered friend," he said. As Edgar suggested, if he claimed to have no cheese, he'd have to go into the village to buy some. And if he had to go to the village to buy some, he would not be around Baroness Von Grumpier, who was already driving him bonkers.

More bonkers than the villagers, and that was saying a lot!

"Cheese it is, cousin," said Baron Von Grump. "Edgar and I will fetch the village's finest cheese. In the meantime, make yourself at home."

4

IF BARON VON GRUMP HAD KNOWN WHAT was going to happen, he never would have told Baroness Von Grumpier to make herself at home. But he didn't know, and so he said it, and then he and Edgar were off on a leisurely walk to the village. He wanted to take as long as he could, so he didn't take his horse and cart. That was another mistake.

. . .

Wolfy followed the trail of cheese crumbs. It led the Junior Monster Scouts and the Little Junior Monster Scouts out to Stargazer's Point. (You may have guessed why it is called that—it is the absolute best place to lie back and watch the stars! Have you ever stargazed? Have you ever looked out into space and just enjoyed all those twinkling stars? Next time you do, see if you can connect the dots and create shapes. Some of those shapes are called *constellations*. Maybe you'll see a dragon, or a two-headed chicken, or maybe even a spider playing a banjo on the back of a hippopotamus!)

Where were we? Oh yes . . .

Wolfy led them out to Stargazer's Point, and sure enough, Boris and the rats were there. They were feasting on cheese and lying about, surrounded by a small collection of garbage.

"Hey, Junior Monster Scouts!" said Boris. His cheeks were packed with cheese. "What brings you all the way out here?"

"You do," said Vampyra.

"Well . . . your littering does," said Franky.

"Yeah," said Wolfy. "What's with all the trash?"

"What, this stuff?" asked Boris. He picked up a fish bone and sniffed it. "Only two weeks old! Man, these villagers throw away the best things."

"What are you doing with it?" asked Vampyra.

"And why is it all over the road?" Franky asked.

"Do you have any idea how hard it is to lug this stuff all the way out here?" asked Boris. "We must have dropped some along the way."

"But you didn't answer our other question," said Wolfy. "What in the world are you doing with all this *trash*?"

"One man's trash is another rat's treasure," said Boris. He tossed the fish bone to one of the other rats. "We're building a nest. Time we moved out of Castle Dracula and built our own home."

"Out of trash?" Fern asked.

"We'd rather refer to it as 'recycled discarded hodgepodge,'" Boris said. "Ain't that right, lads?"

All the other rats nodded and chewed their cheese and occasionally burped.

"I've got an idea," said Franky. "If you help us clean up all the trash—"

"Recycled discarded hodgepodge," Boris said.

"All the recycled discarded hodgepodge," continued Franky, "we'll help you build your nest."

"What do you say, lads?" Boris asked the rats.

"Sounds good to us, boss," said another rat.

The rest of the rats nodded.

"All right, Junior—and Little Junior—Monster Scouts," said Boris. "You've got yourselves a deal."

CHAPTER
5

IF YOU WERE STANDING OUTSIDE Baron Von Grump's windmill at this particular moment, you would have heard an unusual sound. Well, unusual for the windmill. The kind of sound that one would not expect to hear coming from inside Baron Von Grump's windmill: whistling.

Yes, you heard me correctly. Whistling. A cheerful, high-pitched tune being whistled. Of course, we know it was not

Baron Von Grump. He was in the village buying cheese. That must mean that it was none other than Baroness Von Grumpier.

Baroness Von Grumpier whistling? A cheerful whistling? That can't be right. She's supposed to be even grumpier than the baron. And that's a LOT of grump.

But that's exactly who it was, and that's exactly what she was doing. However, it wasn't exactly because she was cheerful. No, her whistling was because she was doing something awful, something she knew would annoy her cousin so much that he would grit his teeth, and flare his nostrils, and maybe even tug on his beard. That made Baroness Von Grumpier smile, and *that* was why she whistled.

"Croak," said Wilma.

The large, warty toad sat on Baron Von Grump's pillow, watching Baroness Von Grumpier as she flitted about the windmill, whistling. That doesn't sound very awful, does it? Well, that is because I haven't told you the rest of what she was doing. Baroness Von Grumpier was gathering all of Baron Von Grump's things and putting them in one big pile.

"I quite agree, Wilma," said Baroness Von Grumpier. "Good riddance to all this rubbish."

"Croak," said Wilma.

"Oh yes, I nearly forgot," said Baroness Von Grumpier. She snatched Baron Von Grump's favorite picture off the wall, the picture of a young (happy) Baron Von Grump playing his violin, and threw it into the pile.

But that's so mean, you might say. See? I told you that she was doing something awful, and that she was a very grumpy, very miserable person. Don't let her whis-

tling fool you. But then she did something even more awful than throwing the picture into the pile.

"Croak," said Wilma.

"Of course! Ah, what would I do without you, Wilma?"

Baroness Von Grumpier picked up Baron Von Grump's most prized possession. His favorite thing in the whole world. The only thing that ever gave him any joy.

You guessed it.

She picked up Baron Von Grump's violin, and without a second thought, she tossed it right over her shoulder. It landed atop the pile with a loud *KER-SPLOING!* as two of the strings snapped.

"Well, that's about everything," said Baroness Von Grumpier.

"Croak," said Wilma.

"Yes, my dear," said Baroness Von Grumpier. "I really am doing him a favor, aren't I? This place was so . . . cluttered. Now then, let's be rid of it all."

Do you remember when I said that it was a mistake that Baron Von Grump and Edgar did not take the horse and cart to reach the village? Baroness Von Grumpier loaded the entire pile of Baron Von Grump's things, including his favorite picture and prized violin, into the cart. And then she and Wilma started off, away from the windmill.

"Let's find a place to dump this garbage,"

said Baroness Von Grumpier. "I simply cannot stand clutter."

And off they went, clattering down the road with a cartful of Baron Von Grump's possessions.

6

BARON VON GRUMP STRODE INTO THE village, much to the surprise of everyone. Villagers closed their doors and shuttered their windows. Anyone who saw him coming went the other way. And can you blame them? The last time Baron Von Grump was in the village, he had hypnotized everyone with his HypnoMirror and Fun House of Fun. Before that, he'd almost flooded the entire village. And then there was the time he cut all of the village power so that they could not celebrate the village's 150th birthday. Oh, and that time he paid Boris and the rats with cheese to scare the villagers away.

As you can see, the villagers were not very fond of Baron Von Grump. But, to be fair, he was not very fond of them either.

Obviously. Unlike Baron Von Grump, however, the villagers were friendly, good-natured people, and so the mayor could not help but tip his hat and say, "Good afternoon, Baron Von Grump. How do you do this fine day?"

"What's so fine about it?" asked Baron Von Grump.

"Caw?" said Edgar. He settled onto Baron Von Grump's shoulder.

"Yes," said Baron Von Grump. "And why should I tell *you* how I am doing today?"

"Well, what brings you to our village on this fine . . . on this *day*?"

"Cheese," said Baron Von Grump.

"But you never come here for cheese," said the mayor. "You only come here when you have a plot, or a plan, or a scheme to ruin our fun."

Baron Von Grump sighed. This was entirely too much talking. Baron Von Grump did not like to talk a lot, or to hear other people talking. *Especially* not to hear other people talking. It was exhausting, and it gave him a headache all the way down to his toes.

Which, come to think about it, might be called a "toe ache." Yes, listening to people talking gave him a toe ache, and now the mayor was saying too many words.

Baron Von Grump wiggled his toes and wished the mayor would just be quiet.

"Cheese," he said. "Three wheels of cheese."

"That's a lot of cheese," said the mayor.

Baron Von Grump groaned. More talking.

"I have a visitor," he said. "My cousin. And if she doesn't get cheese . . ."

Baron Von Grump did not want to think about what she would do if he did not return with cheese. He did not want to even try to imagine her reaction. And so he closed his eyes, opened his mouth, and tried to say a certain word. It was a word he never said. It was a word Baron Von Grump had forgotten how to say. He tried to form the word, but his tongue stuck to the roof of his mouth. He tried again, but his lips stuck together. He tried once more, but he could not quite form the letter *p*, and then . . . Then, with a wheezing, pained expression on his face, he said one single word. A word that echoed through the village. A word that made people stick their heads out their windows and open their doors. A word that shocked the mayor's hat right off his head.

He said . . .

"Please?"

CHAPTER

7

WOLFY, FRANKY, FERN, AND THE REST of the cubs took the left side of the Crooked Trail. Fern and the cubs held the garbage bags while Wolfy and Franky kept the garbage scoopers wound up and scooping litter. On the other side of the Crooked Trail, Vampyra held the bag while Boris and the rats picked up the junk they'd dropped. It was a real team effort.

"A cauldron's less trouble when friends

help stir the bubbles," said Vampyra.

"What does that mean?" Fern asked.

Wolfy held a bag up for a rat to drop in
a sour milk carton.

"My aunt Hemlock says that all the time," said Vampyra. "It means the more people you have helping you, the easier the job is."

"There," said Boris. He dropped the last pile of litter into the bag and wiped his paws clean. "I think that's the last of it."

"I sure hope so," said Wolfy. He pinched his nose shut. "Because this stuff stinks!"

Boris and the rats took a deep breath.

"Sure does!" said Boris. He took a few extra sniffs. "Now let's get this stuff back to Stargazer's Point. We've got a nest to build."

However, while all the scouts and the rats were cleaning up the Crooked Trail, someone else had arrived at Stargazer's Point.

"The perfect spot!" said Baroness Von

Grumpier. "There's already a whole pile of trash here. We might as well just add this junk to the garbage heap."

She backed the cart up and shoveled all of Baron Von Grump's things into the mound of trash that Boris and the rats had piled up. All of it. Even Baron Von Grump's picture and yes—his violin.

KER-SPLOING!!

Another string broke.

Baron Von Grump was halfway home when he stopped. He tilted his head and listened.

"Caw?" asked Edgar.

"Yes, Edgar, I did hear that," said Baron Von Grump. "It did sound like a violin string breaking. The third string, to be exact."

"Caw."

"You're right," said Baron Von Grump. "That's impossible. My dear, dear violin is at home, in our windmill, waiting to be played. Yes, that's exactly what I need. After all this walking, and talking, and listening to that dreadful cousin of mine, there is nothing I want to do more than play my violin."

But when Baron Von Grump got home, he was in for quite a shock. His chair wasn't there. His knickknacks and thingamajigs weren't there. No doodads or decorations. No books, no pillows, no old coats or hangers. Not a cup or a pot or a plate. Not even one candle. Only his cousin Baroness Von Grumpier and her toad, Wilma.

"It's about time you arrived with my cheese," she said. "All this work has left me hungry enough to eat an elephant."

Baron Von Grump dropped the cheese. He dashed up the stairs. He threw open his bedroom door and froze.

"It's not here," he said. "It's gone. My violin! Where is my violin?"

"Oh, that old thing?" asked Baroness Von Grumpier, chewing some cheese (quite loudly, and with her mouth open). "I threw it away. I threw everything away. A little spring-cleaning."

Baron Von Grump balled his hands up. He clenched his teeth. He turned seventeen shades of red.

"YOU THREW AWAY MY VIOLIN!?" he roared.

Baron Von Grump's angry roar washed over the village. It swept up the Crooked Trail. It echoed all the way out to Stargazer's Point.

And then something strange happened.

KER-SPLOING!

The last string on the violin snapped in two.

CRACK!

The glass on Baron Von Grump's picture broke.

The trash pile shuddered. It shook. It formed a giant body made entirely of trash. Baron Von Grump's love for his violin had brought the garbage heap to life!

SNORGLE BELCH GLOBBLE MUCK!

The garbage heap was hungry. Hungry for more trash.

CHAPTER
8

"DID YOU HEAR THAT?" ASKED WOLFY. He had very good ears. He had ears like a wolf.

But you didn't have to have ears like a wolf to have heard what Wolfy heard. The sounds were very loud.

"I heard a KER-SPLOING!" said Franky.

"I heard a CRACK!" said Vampyra.

"And I heard a SNORGLE BELCH GLOBBLE MUCK!" said little Fern.

"That might have been my stomach rumbling," said Boris. "All that work got me hungry for more cheese."

"I don't know, Boris," said Wolfy. "I think it was something else. It sounded like it came from Stargazer's Point."

But they didn't have to go too far to discover what had made those noises.

The walking trash pile was headed right for them. It was made of everything the rats had collected and all of Baron Von Grump's belongings. All that junk had formed into one big, quivering, lumbering pile of trash.

"It can't be!" said Wolfy.

"It is!" said Franky. "But how?"

"Our trash!" cried Boris. "Do you know how long it took us to collect all that?"

"Look out!" Vampyra said.

The trash pile snatched the bags of litter right out of the scouts' hands and dumped everything into its mouth.

"SNORGLE BELCH GLOBBLE MUCK," said the trash heap. "HUNGRY! WANT MORE GARBAGE!"

The giant pile of garbage slid slowly

away from Stargazer's Point, headed for the one place it thought it might find more trash. . . .

"The village!" Vampyra said.

"We've got to warn them!" said Franky.

Wolfy lifted his chin and let out a long, loud howl. Fern and the Little Junior Monster Scouts joined him.

Speaking of the village . . .

Everyone in the village had come out of their homes and their shops at the sound of Baron Von Grump's angry shout. Children stopped playing Snurgle Ball and stared at the windmill. Cows stopped giving milk. Chickens stopped laying eggs. Spiders stopped spinning their webs. Everyone and everything stopped. Sure, Baron Von Grump was cranky, and unfriendly, and occasionally came up with devious plans to chase the villagers away, or make them stop doing things. You know, things like smiling, talking, singing, chewing gum, or playing Snurgle Ball. But nobody had ever heard him shout anything like the shout he had just shouted.

The mayor thought for a moment. He thought back to that morning, when Baron Von Grump had come to buy cheese. But it wasn't the visit, or the cheese, that he was thinking about. He was thinking about what Baron Von Grump had said. About the one word that had knocked the mayor's hat clean off his head.

"Everyone, listen closely," said the mayor. "Everyone knows that Baron Von Grump is cranky at times—"

"All the time," said one villager. "He doesn't even like when we chew gum."

"And we know that he can be unfriendly," said the mayor.

"He chased us away with rats!" said another villager.

"He tried to cancel our birthday party," said a third villager.

"His wild storm blew me right up into the air," said an old woman, knitting. "Rocking chair and all."

"He hypnotized us and made us cluck like chickens and moo like cows," said a farmer, holding a chicken and petting his cow.

"Yes, yes," said the mayor, "but he is our neighbor, and I think he might need our help. I've learned a thing or two from our friends, the Junior Monster Scouts, and—oh, look. Here they are now!"

Wolfy, Franky, Vampyra, Fern, and the Little Junior Monster Scouts cubs raced into the village, waving their arms and shouting.

"Run!" they said. "Everybody, run!"

Boris and the rats were right behind them.

"It's a garbage monster!" the rats cried. "And it's—"

"HUNGRY," said the pile of garbage, now even bigger than it was at Stargazer's Point. "SNORGLE BELCH GLOBBLE MUCK."

56

The trash heap snatched up a fence, and a wagon, and a chimney, and swallowed them all in one gulp.

The villagers panicked. They ran this way and that way and that way and this way, all desperate to get away from the trash heap that looked like it would eat anything in its path.

"Save yourselves!" yelled Boris.

"Run for your lives!" said the mayor.

Vampyra, Wolfy, Franky, Fern, and the Little Junior Monster Scouts stopped running.

Wolfy knelt down next to Fern and the cubs.

"Little Junior Monster Scouts, what's the first scout motto?"

Fern cleared her throat, and she and the rest of the cubs said, "By paw or claw, by tooth or wing, Junior Monster Scouts can do anything."

"That's right, cubs," said Vampyra. "And we have to stop that trash heap."

Franky scratched his bolts. He did that when he was thinking of an idea. He thought about what the trash pile wanted. He thought about something the villagers did not want. He scratched his bolts again.

"I think I have a plan," he said.

"OH, LISTEN TO THOSE VILLAGERS!"
said Baroness Von Grumpier. "Look how
they run this way and that way and that
way and this way. Are they always so lively?"

Baron Von Grump grimaced.

"Unfortunately, yes," he said.

"Who knew this drab place could be so
exciting," said Baroness Von Grumpier. She
clapped her hands together in joy.

"Croak," said Wilma.

"Yes, of course," said Baroness Von Grumpier. "You may lick all the cheese you would like."

Baron Von Grump couldn't take any more. First his cousin had thrown away all his things, including his violin. Then,

because of her, the entire village had become even noisier than it already was. And now—now she was going to let that warty toad lick all the cheese? Who wants to eat cheese after anyone has licked it? Especially a warty toad!

Let's try an experiment. Get yourself a little snack . . . maybe a piece of cheese, a cracker, or a cookie. Maybe a crisp apple slice or a piece of pepperoni. Now lick it. A lot. Give it a real wet, slobbery lick. Make sure someone sees you. Now offer them a bite. You might say, *Would you like a bite of my cracker? The one I just licked?* How did they react? They probably did not want a bite, did they? And if they did, well, I'd keep an eye on them if I were you. They might be going around licking all the other food in your house. And that's just gross.

Baron Von Grump stomped down the stairs. He threw open the door, stepped out of the windmill, and slammed the door behind him.

"Caw?" asked Edgar, circling Baron Von Grump.

"To the village," said Baron Von Grump. "To see what all this fuss is about."

"Caw caw?"

"And then what?" Baron Von Grump said, repeating Edgar's question. "We'll put a stop to it. No more noise, and no more entertainment for Baroness Von Grump-ier. If we make things less exciting, maybe she'll leave."

"Caw!" said Edgar.

"Yes," said Baron Von Grump, "and take her toad-licked cheese with her!"

Allow me to interrupt the story for a minute. I thought this might be a good time to tell you that "toad-licked" became a very common saying in the village for things you didn't like. For example, you might say, "Mom, I don't want any toad-licked lima beans," or maybe "I don't root for that toad-licked team." Maybe even "I happen to prefer strawberry jelly over toad-licked grape jelly."

But now back to the story.

Baron Von Grump marched right down to the village, with Edgar flying beside him.

When he reached the village, he froze.

The giant trash heap ambled along,

upending rubbish bins and trash carts right into its mouth.

"It can't be," said Baron Von Grump.

But that is not what caught Baron Von Grump's attention.

"Caw!" said Edgar.

Baron Von Grump could not believe his eyes.

There, in the middle of the creature, was his violin.

CHAPTER
10

FRANKY EXPLAINED HIS PLAN TO WOLFY,
Vampyra, Fern, and the rest of the cubs.

"Paws and claws in," said Wolfy.

The Junior and Little Junior Monster
Scouts all put their hands together.

"When someone else is in trouble . . . ,"
said Vampyra.

"We help them out on the double!" said
Wolfy, Franky, Fern, and the Little Junior
Monster Scouts.

Wolfy and Vampyra grabbed the last two carts of garbage and pushed them away from the village, but not before Fern and the cubs filled a few sacks with trash.

"Hey," said Boris, stopping to catch his breath. All that running in circles, screaming, had tired him out. "Where are you going with all that trash?"

"Stargazer's Point," said Vampyra. "See if you can find any more garbage lying around, and bring it there!"

"You heard her," Boris said to the other rats. "Let's do what we do best!"

"Eat cheese?" asked a rat.

"No, the other thing," said Boris. "Gather garbage."

While Vampyra and Wolfy pushed those

gross, yucky, fly-ridden piles of trash to Stargazer's Point, Fern and the cubs dropped a trail of litter along the way. Some dirty napkins here, a rusted tomato sauce can there. A broken plate here, a bent bicycle tire there. They did this all the way from the village to Stargazer's Point.

While the rats and the Junior Monster Scouts were busy moving trash, the trash pile was busy moving deeper into the village. It slurped old slop. It guzzled gristle and fat. It chewed on old tires and munched on mold-covered melon rinds. It got bigger, and bigger, and bigger with every mouthful of garbage.

Franky stood in the middle of the village, dangling a slop-stained old boot that someone had put out in the trash.

"Um, Mister Trash Pile?" said Franky. He took a step backward. "Excuse me?" He took another nervous step backward. "I have a very smelly, very icky old boot you might be interested in."

The trash heap reached for the boot, but Franky pulled it away.

"HUNGRY," said the trash heap.

"And there's more where this came from," said Franky.

"MORE?" asked the trash heap. "SNORGLE BELCH GLOBBLE MUCK."

"But you have to follow me," said Franky.

Franky took a few steps backward along the trail of garbage Fern and the cubs had left. Every time the trash heap reached a piece of garbage, it scooped it up and gobbled it down.

"YUMMY YUMMY FOR MY TUMMY,"
said the trash heap.

"Speaking of tummies," said Baron Von Grump, suddenly appearing from behind the trash heap, "you have something of mine in yours."

"Where did *he* come from?" Wolfy asked.

"From behind the trash pile," Boris whispered.

Wolfy rolled his eyes. "I *know* that," he said. "What I meant was—"

"SNORGLE?"

"Caw!" said Edgar.

"BELCH GLOBBLE!"

"And I want it back!" said Baron Von Grump.

"GLOBBLE MUCK!" roared the trash heap.

Baron Von Grump rolled his coat sleeves up and marched forward.

Franky waved the old boot around,

trying to get the trash heap's attention.

"No, over here!" Franky said. "Baron Von Grump, don't take another step!"

But Baron Von Grump did not listen. He took not one, but *two*, steps and . . .

GULP!

Baron Von Grump was gone. Swallowed up and in the belly of the trash heap.

BEFORE YOU BEGIN TO WORRY, I WANT to assure you that Baron Von Grump was okay. He wasn't hurt, not in any way. He was a bit stinky, and a bit slimy, and he may have had a banana peel on his shoulder and some old pudding on his sleeve, but otherwise he was fine. In fact, he was rather happy.

Happy? Happy to be swallowed by a trash heap and surrounded by piles of gross garbage? That can't be right. But it was. You see, inside the trash heap it was quiet. Smelly, yes. But quiet. And there was his old picture, the one of young Baron Von Grump playing his violin. Speaking of violins, there it was, his most favorite thing in the whole world.

Baron Von Grump picked up his violin and pulled it close.

"I'll have you fixed up in no time," he said. "New strings, a bit of polish, and a nice tuning."

And so, you see, Baron Von Grump was quite fine, and quite happy.

Edgar, however, was not.

"Caw, caw!" he said. He flew in circles around the trash heap.

The trash heap spun in circles, following the frantic crow.

Edgar was very concerned about his best friend being swallowed whole by a giant trash heap. Wouldn't you be? Of course you would. That's because you're a good friend, and so was Edgar.

"Edgar, I know you're upset," said Franky. "But together we might just be able to save the baron."

"Caw?"

"Take this old boot and lure the trash heap to Stargazer's Point," said Franky.

"Caw!"

"I know it's gross," said Franky. "And yes, it smells like a hundred sweaty toes stepped in a puddle of old milk."

"Caw?"

"I'll be there shortly," said Franky.

"There's one more thing I need to do."

Edgar took the old, slop-stained boot in his beak. He flew above the trash heap, swooping down every once in a while to dangle it in front of the trash heap's mouth.

"SNORGLE BELCH GLOBBLE MUCK!" said the trash heap.

But no matter how much the trash heap tried, it just could not get that old boot. Edgar was too quick. With loops and swoops and dips and twirls, Edgar led that giant trash heap all the way out to Stargazer's Point.

Wolfy stood atop a large rock at Stargazer's Point. He had been keeping an eye out for the trash heap.

"Here they come!" he said.

The trash heap was the biggest they had seen it yet. It was five times the size it had been when they had first seen it. It was headed straight for them, chasing Edgar.

"What's Edgar doing here?" asked Vampyra. "And what's he doing with that old boot?"

"And where's Franky?" Fern asked.

"What do you want us to do with all this sweet, wonderful, stinky old garbage?" Boris asked. He and the rats had armfuls of trash.

Vampyra remembered Franky's plan.

"Put it in one nice pile, right here," she said.

"Yoo-hoo," called Wolfy. "Over here!"

Edgar dropped the old boot atop the new pile of garbage.

The trash heap lumbered forward.

"HUNGRY!"

It opened its mouth wide and gobbled up every bit of the trash they'd collected, including the old boot.

It grew in size again. It grew three *more* times. It shook. It shivered. It rumbled and grumbled and quivered and quaked.

"SNORGLE BELCH GLOBBLE MUCK!" it said. And then it let out the loudest, grossest, smelliest burp anyone had ever heard.

BURRRRRRRRRRRRRRRRRRRRRRRRP.

It was so loud and so long that it shot Baron Von Grump right out of the trash heap's belly. He landed with a splat, still holding his dear violin.

"MORE GARBAGE EAT!" said the trash heap.

It loomed over the Junior and Little Junior

Monster Scouts, Baron Von Grump, Edgar, and Boris and the rats.

It seemed there was no stopping the trash heap.

It was still hungry.

CHAPTER
12

BARONESS VON GRUMPIER WATCHED THE village from the old windmill.

"Where's all the noise?" she asked.

"Croak," said Wilma.

"Where's all the fuss and the ruckus?" asked Baroness Von Grumpier.

"Croak," said Wilma.

"Things were just getting exciting!" said Baroness Von Grumpier. "And now it's too boring, too drab."

Baroness Von Grumpier had watched the villagers. One by one, the villagers had stepped out of their homes with trash buckets and boxes. They had followed Franky and the mayor out of the village.

"They've all left," said Baroness Von Grumpier. "They've followed that Junior Monster Scout away from the village!"

"Croak?"

"I have no idea where." She leaned out the window and shouted, "I demand you come back!"

Franky and the villagers might have heard her if they had been closer to the village *and* if that were not the *exact* time that the trash heap let out the longest, biggest BURRRRRRRRRRRRRRRRRRRRRRP!

The village was now quiet and empty. This did not make Baroness Von Grumpier happy. Not one bit.

Franky led the villagers and their trash back to Stargazer's Point, just as the trash heap was looming over his friends.

"Excuse me, trash heap?" Franky said. He tugged at his bolts. He did this sometimes, when he was nervous.

"SNORGLE?"

"Are you still hungry?" Franky asked.

The trash heap nodded.

"SNORGLE?"

The mayor stepped forward and placed a bucket of garbage from his very own house in front of the trash heap. It swallowed it all up and smiled.

"We have more for you," said the mayor. (Remember that thing that Franky knew the villagers did *not* want? That's right! They didn't want their garbage. It was garbage, after all!)

"HUNGRY," said the trash heap.

"We know you're hungry," said Wolfy.

"But you can't just go around scaring everyone and eating everything that you see," said Vampyra.

The trash heap opened its mouth. It closed its mouth. It looked at the empty bucket the mayor had given it. It thought that it had been very kind and generous of the mayor to offer it trash from his own house.

"SNORGLE MUCK," said the trash heap. It
drooped its shoulders and bowed its head.

"What if the villagers brought you their

trash every week?" Franky asked. "Would you promise not to bother the village?"

"GLOBBLE MUCK!" The trash heap nodded again.

"Wait a minute," said Boris. "That's supposed to be our trash!"

"That is why we'd like to partner with you rats," said the mayor. "Each week, you collect the garbage from the village and bring it out to our friend, the trash heap. In return, you get to keep some of it. Is that fair?"

Boris and the rats put their heads together.

"Throw in the occasional block of cheese, and you've got a deal," said Boris.

"Done," said the mayor. "Trash heap, is that okay with you?"

"GLOBBLE MUCK," said the trash heap. It nodded yet again and smiled.

"Then it's decided!" said the mayor. "The village will be cleaner, the trash heap won't be hungry, and the rats will help and be helped in return. Oh, you clever Junior Monster Scouts. Always thinking of just the right thing to save the day!"

"What about Baron Von . . . Grump?" Wolfy asked.

Baron Von Grump was nowhere to be found. In all the excitement, it seemed he had slipped away with his violin and Edgar.

I wonder where he went, or what he was up to.

Hmmmm . . .

But let's focus on the Junior Monster

Scouts. They had had a very long day of picking up litter, and it was almost time for their Junior Monster Scouts scout meeting back at Castle Dracula.

13

". . . AND THEN THE TRASH HEAP SAID, 'SNORGLE BELCH GLOBBLE MUCK,'" Fern said, "and we gave it all the trash that the villagers collected from along the Crooked Trail, and then it was happy!"

"Well, that is some tale!" said Frankenstein. He was Franky's dad and one of their scout leaders.

"Now the village is cleaner," said Franky.

"And smells better too!" said Wolfy.

"And even the rats have a job," said Vampyra. "They bring the village's garbage to the trash heap, and they get to keep some. They built their own little nest out there and keep the trash heap company."

"I'm going to miss those little guys running around the castle's basement," said Dracula. He was Vampyra's dad and another one of their scout leaders.

"Did anyone ever find out where Baron Von Grump went?" Wolf Man asked. He was Wolfy's father, and yes, he was also a scout leader.

"No idea," said Franky.

"Well, I know one thing," said Frankenstein. "For all your hard work in cleaning up the Crooked Trail, you Monster Scouts,

Junior *and* Little, earned your Clean Up the Community Merit Badges."

"And for helping the village, the trash heap, and the rats," said Wolf Man, "you get your Good Neighbor Merit Badges."

Dracula pinned the merit badges onto the scouts' sashes.

"Well done," Dracula said. "Now, why

don't we all go up to the tallest tower and look at the stars? Igor Senior and Igor Junior just installed a new telescope, and it'll give you a chance to work on your Astronomy Merit Badges without all the stink."

The Monster Scouts giggled and followed Dracula to the tallest tower, where a very large telescope was aimed at the moon.

If they had moved the telescope a bit to the right and a little down, they would have answered Wolf Man's earlier question about where Baron Von Grump had gone.

Because at that very moment he was standing on the newly named Trash Heap Point. And his arms were not empty. Edgar was with him, and Edgar's beak was not empty.

"Good evening, trash heap," said Baron

Von Grump. "My good friend Edgar and I were wondering if you might like a midnight snack?"

The trash heap smiled.

"SNURGLE!"

Baron Von Grump grinned his slimiest grin and gladly gave the trash heap . . .

"MY LUGGAGE!" SHRIEKED BARONESS Von Grumpier. "My satchel! My trunk, and my bags, and my box. They're all gone!"

"Croak?" asked Wilma.

"They were here just yesterday!" said Baroness Von Grumpier. She swept through the windmill in a tizzy. "Baron Von Grump, have you any idea where my things are? My luggage? My satchel? My trunk, or my bags, or my box?"

Baron Von Grump sat in his empty room, on an empty crate, tuning his violin. It had been polished and had four new strings. A single picture hung on the wall. I think you know exactly which picture . . . the one of young Baron Von Grump happily playing his violin. It hung perfectly straight on one single nail, just the way he liked it.

"I haven't the slightest idea," he said, with a smile that slipped from ear to ear like a wiggling worm.

"Caw," said Edgar, shrugging his wings.

Baron Von Grump winked at his friend, the crow. Then Baron Von Grump drew the bow across the strings, and the violin made a beautiful sound.

Baroness Von Grumpier harrumphed and

slammed the door so hard that Baron Von Grump's picture tilted just a bit off-center.

"You can't get rid of me that easy, cousin!" said Baroness Von Grumpier, stomping down the stairs as loud as she could.

Baron Von Grump could not hear her over his violin playing. And that was just the way he liked it. But don't worry—he threw in a grumpy scowl, just for good measure. After all, his name is Baron Von Grump.

SNORGLE BELCH GLOBBLE MUCK!

· ACKNOWLEDGMENTS ·

Thank you to the usual suspects, for your support: Jess, my wife, best friend, and absolute love. You inspire me and challenge me, babe! Shane, Logan, Sawyer, Ainsley, Zach, and Braeden—you're always part of the journey. Becca, Josh, Maddie, and Lena for cheering me on and celebrating every book I write.

I'm super grateful for my awesome agent, Jennifer Soloway, who champions my work and believes in me! I'm lucky to be your author, Jennifer. Thank you.

These books would not be what they are without the tireless work and incredible vision of my editor, Karen Nagel. Thank you, Karen! What a cool universe we've built!

A great big thank you to Ethan, for your wonderful illustrations. I'd like to recognize the entire Aladdin team for all the hard work they put into making the Junior Monster Scouts books so great—the design department, copy editors, marketing . . . all of you wonderful behind-the-scenes people, THANK YOU!

Thank you to my mom and dad for giving a creative young boy the books, games, crayons, and coloring books he needed to feed an overactive imagination.

And finally, thank YOU, the reader. Without you, there wouldn't be books on the shelf, right? So keep reading . . . Keep turning those pages and exploring worlds. Untold stories await you!

100

JUNIOR MONSTER SCOUT
· HANDBOOK ·

The Junior Monster Scout oath:

I promise to be nice, not scary. To help, not harm.

To always try to do my best. I am a monster, but

I am not mean. I am a Junior Monster Scout!

Junior Monster Scout mottos:

By paw or claw, by tooth or wing, Junior
  Monster Scouts can do anything!
Never say "never" when friends work together!
By tooth or wing, by paw or claw, a Junior
  Monster Scout does it all!
When someone else is in trouble, we help
  them out on the double!

Junior Monster Scout laws:

Be Kind—A scout treats others the way
they want to be treated.

Be Friendly—A scout is open to everyone, no matter how different they are.

Be Helpful—A scout goes out of their
way to do good deeds for others . . . without expecting a reward.

Be Careful—A scout thinks about what they say or do *before* they do it.

Be a Good Listener—A scout listens to what others have to say.

Be Brave—A scout does what is right, even if they are afraid, and a scout makes the right decisions . . . even if no one else does.

Be Trustworthy—A scout does what they say they will do, even if it is difficult.

Be Loyal—A scout is a good friend and will always be there for you when you need them.

Junior Monster Scout badges in this book:
Clean Up the Community Merit Badge
Good Neighbor Merit Badge

READ ON FOR A PEEK AT
NIGHT FRIGHTS, A BRAND-NEW SPOOKY
SERIES FROM JOE McGEE.

". . . And his mustache was all that remained."

Mr. Noffler leaned against the edge of his desk and watched the class. They were silent for a moment. Their eyes were wide. None of the students knew whether or not to believe what they'd just heard.

Every kid in Wolver Hollow grew up going through the same weird routine on October

19, but until now, they never knew why. Every October 19, the town shut down before dusk.

Shops closed.

Parents made their children stay inside.

Curtains were drawn.

And doors were bolted.

Every year, men who were normally clean-shaven grew mustaches in preparation for October 19. Women and children took their fake mustaches out of the drawer and taped them above their lips. Parents made a game of it, but their eyes were filled with fear.

When children would ask why they had to wear mustaches, or what Mommy was so afraid of, it was always the same answer: "You're too young" or "It's nothing, just a silly old legend." But now that they were in fifth grade, they were finally learning the truth. They were finally going to hear about the legend of October 19.

"And that is today's local history lesson," said Mr. Noffler. He clapped his hands and sat down.

Parker frowned. That couldn't be it, he thought. He had the feeling that Mr. Noffler was leaving out all of the good parts. He hadn't told them why it was all such a big deal in the first place. He hadn't told them why they locked their doors and wore fake mustaches. Parker sensed a mystery, and he wanted answers. He was not about to let Mr. Noffler stop there. Not when he was so close to learning the truth. Parker leaned forward at his desk and raised his hand as high as he could.

"Yes, Parker?" said Mr. Noffler. He set down his marker and adjusted his glasses.

"How *big* was the explosion?" asked Parker.

"So big," said Mr. Noffler, "that it rattled houses and broke windows for miles around. It left a crater in the ground large enough that our entire school could fit inside of it!"

The class murmured in amazement.

"Well, how did the gunpowder explode?" Parker asked.

Mr. Noffler tapped his upper lip, like he always did when he was considering his answer. Mr. Noffler did not normally have a mustache, but, like everyone else, this week he did. October 19 was only one day away. He crossed his arms and stared at Parker.

"That's a great question, Parker," said Mr.

Noffler. "No one ever quite figured out what caused the unfortunate black powder incident that vaporized poor old Bockius Beauregard. It was labeled an accident."

"Vaporized?" Parker asked.

"Vaporized," said Mr. Noffler. "Well . . . mostly. As I said—"

"The mustache," said Lucas, Parker's best friend. "It survived."

"Yes, the mustache," said Mr. Noffler. "The magnificent mustache of Bockius Beauregard. It was the envy of every man in town."

"That must have been some mustache," said Gilbert Blardle, doodling mustaches in the margin of his notebook.

"Indeed it was," said Mr. Noffler. "There never was another mustache quite so magnificent ever recorded again in Wolver Hollow."

"Who keeps track of mustaches?" asked Lucas.

"This is the weirdest town ever," said Parker.

"Some say that mustache had a life of its own," continued Mr. Noffler. "Some say that that is why it returns from the grave every year on the anniversary of Bockius Beauregard's unfortunate explosion. Nobody knows for certain. Nobody dares to go looking. And so, it remains . . . a mystery."

A mystery! Parker's eyes lit up. He knew it!

"Wait," said Parker. "Did you just say that the mustache returns? From the grave?"

Mr. Noffler smiled and stood up from his desk. "I did."